Beautiful In My Eyes

Eyes

J. Adams

J. Adams

Jewel of the West Publishing

ISBN-13: 978-0615659923

ISBN-10: 0615659926

Library of Congress Control Number: 2012911177

To Tami T.

one of my many kindred spirits.

J. Adams

Believe me, if all those endearing young charms,

Which I gaze on so fondly today,
Were to change by tomorrow and fleet in my arms,
Like fairy wings fading away
Thou wouldst still be adored, as this moment thou art,
Let thy loveliness fade as it will;
And around the dear ruin each wish of my heart
Would entwine itself verdantly still.

It is not while beauty and youth are thine own,
And thy cheeks unprofaned by a tear,
That the fervor and faith of a soul can be known,
To which time will but make thee more dear.
No, the heart that has truly loved never forgets,
But as truly loves on to the close:
As the sunflower turns on her god when he sets
The same look which she turned when he rose.

Thomas Moore

IV

Charlotte, North Carolina

Mama, I don't know how to do this anymore. It's just too hard. It's hard on me, and on him most of all.

Having slept curled up in a comfortable recliner in my father's bedroom, I awaken at the sound of his alarm. I watch him where he lay, staring at the ceiling, willing himself to get up.

It is the same every year. He turns over and gently places his hand on the empty pillow, a single tear slipping across the bridge of his nose.

To the rest of the world, this day is the same as any other, but for Dad, this day is still one of great pain and sadness. It marks the three-year anniversary of my mother's death. Emotionally, Dad has good and bad days, but their wedding anniversary is usually the hardest. So while my husband takes care of our little boy, I come over to be here for Dad. I still miss Mama more than I can say, but she had been my father's whole world.

Grabbing the pillow, he clutches it tightly to his chest as the first sob rolls forth and I go to him.

"Oh, Giselle, I miss her so much."

"I know, Dad," I whisper, wrapping my arms around him and rocking him gently. "I know you do."

"I thought it would be easier by now, but it's not. She was my whole life."

"And you were hers," I whisper, emotion lodged in my throat. "She loved you so much, Dad."

He lets me hold him for a few minutes, soaking in my comfort like a lost child. Finally drawing back a little, he nods and wipes his eyes, fresh tears quickly marking new tracks down his face.

"She wants you to be happy. I know she does."

"I know." Heaving a deep sigh, he smiles sadly. "I believe that, too. She was, and still is one of the most selfless people I have ever known. And you take after her."

"I don't know if I can ever reach her level."

"You already have." He presses a kiss to my forehead and holds me close another moment. "I will be all right, honey." He releases me, his smile brightening. "Thank you for being here for me. And thank Julian for sacrificing you yet again."

"I will." I press a hand to his stubbly, handsome face and brush the lightly-graying blond hair from his forehead. "I will always be here for you, Dad. I promise."

"Yes, I know. God gave us a wonderful gift when He sent you to us. Our little miracle. Though not so little anymore."

"Well, no matter how old I get, I will always be your little girl."

"I know. And I really will be all right, starting right now. I will make it through this. Thank you for being so strong for me."

"Me? Sometimes I don't feel strong. Sometimes I feel far from it."

"You are made of tough stuff, Giselle. After all, you are Jack and Janice Mason's stunningly-beautiful daughter. Our blood runs through your veins. There is no trial you can't handle."

Beautiful. I close my eyes as he kisses my brow. *Oh, Dad, if you only knew. I don't feel stunningly-beautiful. Not even beautiful. The small bit of vanity I once possessed has been blown away like the flame of a candle in the wind.*

"Thank you, Dad."

Chapter 1

Beauty is truth, truth beauty -- that is all ye know on earth, and all ye need to know.

John Keats

Two months later

Standing just inside the patio door, I watch Dad kneel on the grass and hold his arms out to his grandson.

"Come on, Aidan! Walk to Grampa! Come on, you can do it!"

Little Aidan takes step after tiny step until he makes it to Dad's arms. "Good job, buddy! Good job!"

I smile as I continue watching two of the three most important men in my life. And a moment later I am wrapped in warmth as the third's arms slip around my waist. I lean back and snuggle against him, relishing his familiar comforting embrace. "You're home early."

"Aye," Julian replies, kissing my cheek. "Steve didnae need as much help with the inventory as I thought. We got everythin' don' quickly. An' I postponed the readin' til next week."

I nuzzle my face against his cheek before turning in his arms. "Well, I'm glad you're here, and the young mothers that religiously bring their kids in for story time will just have to wait a little longer to see my Scottish knight in a kilt. You should remind them to bring bibs. Wouldn't want them drooling all over the place."

"Aye, a couple o them tried ta follow me home an' I had ta maneuver a bit ta lose them." He smiles, tightening his embrace. "Good thin' we're acquainted with half the cops in the area or I would be gettin' regular speedin' tickets because I'm always in such a hurry ta get home ta ye."

"It *is* a good thing," I whisper just as he touches his lips to mine. Our kiss quickly deepens as his warm mouth make thorough work of heating me to the core. Whenever he kisses me, I lose all sense of time and place, and the only thing that surpasses it is when we make love. His affections never fail to affect me this way.

Hearing a throat clearing, we draw apart a little and turn, meeting Dad's wide grin, his grandson sitting on his shoulders. "Careful or you two might set the place on fire."

I snort. "Ooooh, that would definitely give the neighbors something to talk about."

Julian kisses my cheek and fingers one of the curls in my ponytail. "An' I'm alwa's willin' ta do ma part in educatin' the neighbors aboot the hazards of marryin' a gorgeous, caramel-skinned goddess."

Dad laughs. "I'm in complete agreement."

Hearing the deeper meaning in his words, I smile, squeezing his hand. Dad had endured some painful things when he married Mama. In his wealthy family, marrying a black woman just wasn't done. But he had been willing to sacrifice everything for my mother's hand, and sacrifice he did. I also know he has no regrets and wouldn't have changed a thing.

"Dada," Aidan says, holding his arms out to Julian, practically jumping into his.

"There's ma boy! Did ye hav' a good time with Grampa?"

"Of course," Dad says, tickling Aidan's stomach, drawing a delightful giggle from him.

"I think it's nap time for you," I say, brushing the hair from his brow.

"I'll take him up," Julian offers.

"Thanks." I blow a kiss goodbye to the tired little boy, marveling at how much he favors his father. I'm sure he will be the major crush of a lot of teenage girls when he is older. Smiling at the thought, I grab a pitcher of lemonade from the fridge. "Would you like a glass, Dad?"

"Sure."

"So, what do you have planned today?" I ask, taking a seat at the table. Noticing his slightly stressed look, I place my hand over his. "What is it?"

"Well, you won't believe this, but my mother called me today."

I almost drop my glass of lemonade. "What? Are you serious?"

"Completely," he says tonelessly. "She called me this morning and said she and Father would like to see me."

"Wow!"

"Yeah, tell me about it."

Dad hasn't spoken with his parents in over twenty years. They never accepted Mama, or me when I was born, according to Dad. He had received a sizable trust from his parents when he turned twenty-one, so he has never been in need of money, which never really mattered to him, anyway because he has always liked to work. But he had been pretty hurt when they chose not to be a part of his life. He'd almost felt like it was a payoff.

Dad told me that for a short while he tried to stay in contact with them, but they wouldn't even acknowledge him. So he finally stopped trying, convinced it was hopeless. He and his parents lived in the same city and they wouldn't even see him. And all of this was because they had issues with interracial marriage. Still, through it all, Dad never stopped loving Mama, and she never stopped loving him. In the end, their love won.

"Did she say what they wanted?" I ask, bewildered.

"Not a word. And you know, she almost sounded desperate."

Dad sips his lemonade. "I know we don't have the greatest relationship in the world, but they are still my parents. I think I owe them this much. As for plans for the rest of the day, I guess it all depends on how things go there."

I squeeze his hand. "Are you going to be okay?"

He turns his hand over, clasping mine and smiles. "Don't worry. I'll be fine."

"I don't think I can help it. I love you, Dad. I don't want you to be hurt."

He sighs. "And I won't be." He takes a final sip of lemonade before standing. "I'd better go."

I quickly stand and hug him, holding onto him a moment. "Please call me or come by afterward. You know I'll be worried until you do."

He presses a kiss to my brow. "I promise I will."

Chapter 2

Beauty is the mark God sets on virtue. Every natural action is graceful; every heroic act is also decent, and causes the place and the bystanders to shine.

Ralph Waldo Emerson

I put my book away, realizing that trying to read is futile, and pace the floor nervously, anxiously waiting to hear from Dad. I started reading the story earlier this week and

11

have been trying to get it finished, but right now I can't concentrate, and after reading the same paragraph over and over again, I give up. I'm so worried about Dad. Yes, he is a grown man, but he is my dad and I can't help my feelings.

What in the world would they want to talk to him about? The same question keeps rolling through my mind. *For over twenty years they've had nothing to say to him and now suddenly, out of the blue, they want to see him?*

Dad has been through so much and I can't bear the thought of him being hurt again. I have a Mama Bear streak when it comes to him, and I silently pray he is okay.

We have definitely got to get him married, Mama.

I head up to the playroom to check on Aidan. Finding him contently playing with his blocks, I decide to try and kill some time by working on a quilt I have been tying to give a friend at her baby shower. I have only been at it for a few minutes when the doorbell rings. Springing to my feet, I almost knock over a chair as I dash down the stairs to answer the door, praying it is Dad.

"Dad," I sigh, pulling him into the house. "I've been so worried. Is everything all right? What's going on? What did they want? Why–"

"Everything is fine," he interrupts. "Everything is just fine." He wraps an arm around my shoulders, guiding me to the sofa. "I have a lot to tell you."

Mentally muzzling myself, I quietly listen as Dad fills me in, giving me all the details of his visit with his parents.

"The first few minutes were strained. I don't think either of us knew what to say. But they soon opened up and apologized to me for shutting me out. They told me how sorry they were for turning their back on me. And Giselle, I honestly didn't know what to say. To say I was in complete shock is putting it mildly."

He pauses, wiping his eyes and I can read his every emotion in his expression. His watery smile draws my own tears to the surface.

"They want to try and make up for lost time–time they know they will never get back. And they want to meet their granddaughter and her family."

I am floored. "I can't believe it! They really want to see us?"

"They really do," he assures me.

After all these years, I will get to meet my grandparents for the first time. I can't help feeling a little sad that Mama can't be here to experience this. She had longed to meet Dad's parents, to be a part of a family, something she hadn't had for years since her parents and older brother died the year I was born.

"Giselle," Dad says, drawing me from my thoughts, "Are you going to be okay with this?"

"Of course I am," I say, wanting to put his mind at ease. "I'm actually looking forward to it." Inside I am still a little wary, but I know how important this is to him. I know things will work out.

Julian enters the living room a while later, having finished some paperwork from the office, and Dad fills him in on the details of his visit with his parents. Smiling, Julian says, "Our family is extendin'. We're bein' verra blessed." And I agree completely.

A moment later I hear Aidan chattering behind the safety. "He must be bored with the blocks," I say, getting up. When I reach the top of the stairs, he gives me that irresistible grin of his.

"You know you can get a woman to do just about anything with that grin, don't you?" I lift him from behind the gate and take him downstairs. "You are taking after your da, charming women the way you do."

"An' there's nothin' wrong with tha', darlin'?" Julian boldly states. "Is there?" He takes his son and soon both men are on the floor, tickling and wrestling with him.

Enjoying the sight, my gaze shifts to my father. The joy radiating from him is contagious. He smiles at me, confirming his happiness.

It has been a good day.

A few days later, I am about to get out of the shower when the phone rings. Grabbing a towel, I run to answer it.

"Is this Giselle?"

"Yes, it is."

"Hey, this is Mark Hayes."

"Mark! How have you been, guy?"

"I've been great. How about you?"

"I'm good," I answer, excited to hear from our friend. We haven't talked to Mark in about a year, but we think of him often and wish he didn't live so far away. He used to live just down the road from us, but a job change took him back home to Salt Lake City, Utah. I am sure his family has enjoyed having him home again.

"So what have you been up to?" I ask, sitting on the edge of the bed.

"Oh, not a whole lot. Just work and finishing up school. That has kept me pretty busy."

"I'd imagine so. I hope you're leaving some time on your social calendar."

Mark laughs. "Actually, someone has been keeping my social calendar pretty filled."

"I knew it! What's her name and how did you meet her?"

"Her name is Sara and I met her in one of my classes. She's a petite brunette with big blue eyes and a dazzling smile."

"So, how long have you two been dating?"

"Oh, for about six months now, and we've been engaged for about three weeks."

"Really?" I squeal. "That's awesome, Mark. Congratulations!"

"Thanks."

"So when is the big day?"

"Well, that's why I'm calling. We've set it for June seventeenth."

"Wow, six weeks! That's soon, but hey, you know me. I think when you find the right person, the sooner the better."

"So do we. I plan to call your dad and ask him about this too, but it would really mean a lot to me if you guys could come out for the wedding. I know that doesn't give you much time to–"

"Yes!" I cut him off. "We would be honored to come to your wedding."

"Great! It's gonna be so awesome having you guys here."

"I'm looking forward to it. And you go ahead and call Dad on his cell. He went in to work early this morning and I'm sure he will be excited to hear, too."

"Okay, I will. My family's home is large with plenty of room, so you will all have a place to stay. I told them I planned to invite you and they are looking forward to meeting you guys."

"Thanks, Mark. That means a lot."

"Truthfully, Giselle, your names were at the top of my list. You guys have been in my thoughts for quite some time now. But every time I have planned to call you, something has come up."

"Hey, I can understand that. Don't worry about it."

"I'm glad everything is going okay with you. I guess I'll call Jack and tell him my news."

"You do that. I know he will be glad to hear from you."

"I'll call you back this weekend with more details."

"Sounds good. Congratulations again, Mark. You take care of yourself."

"You too, Giselle."

I smile as I hang up the phone. I love hearing good news, and Mark's upcoming marriage is definitely cause to celebrate.

I finish getting dressed. Sitting at the vanity in the bathroom, I run a brush through my damp hair, blinking back the tears as a large clump of hair collects in the bristles. Cleaning the brush is becoming routine, one that is making me more down with each passing day. Before the hair loss started, I had always been pleased with my long, naturally-curly locks and had taken pride in the styling versatility, but each time I pull the brush away and find it full, my sadness increases tenfold. I only hope and pray that it doesn't get bad enough for Julian to notice because he loves my hair so much.

By some strange good fortune, I never seem to lose hair when Julian touches it, nor when we are intimate, and I thank the heavens every day for that. I've tried different shampoos, conditioners and other styling products, but nothing has helped or made any amount of difference.

Well, it isn't as bad as some women. At least not yet. Rather than dwell on it, I style the curls in an attractive up-do and do my best to change the course of my thoughts to something positive.

With gratitude in my heart, I think on this past week. It has been an amazing one.

Dad took us to his parent's home a couple of days ago and things went really well. As soon as we stepped through their door, Jim and Donna Mason swept me into a loving embrace and the apprehension I felt quickly faded away. My grandmother and grandfather spent the better part of the evening getting to know us, and they totally fell in love with little Aidan. The memory of the love and acceptance I felt from them brings tears to my eyes even now. It was an amazing visit and Julian and I are glad to have had the opportunity to get to know them.

And now we are privileged to travel to Utah for Mark's wedding.

Despite my other concern, it has indeed been a good week.

Chapter 3

The beauty that addresses itself to the eyes is only the spell of the moment; the eye of the body is not always that of the soul.

George Sand

*G*rabbing a couple of potholders, I take the last batch of bread from the oven. I baked eight small loaves, five of which will go to friends. After wrapping one in a new dish towel, I quickly head upstairs to change out of my flour-covered shirt, then fix my hair, and stop by the den to let Julian know I am leaving.

"John and I are separating."

Covering my mouth, I attempt to hide my shock. "I can't believe it! What happened?" I ask, squeezing my friend Libby's hand.

"Truthfully, I don't know. We have been struggling for a while now. And the simple fact is, though I want our marriage to work, John doesn't. It takes two and I have given it all I've got. I can't do it alone anymore and I'm tired of trying. I asked John if there is someone else. He says no, but I'm not so sure. I mean, I know my age is starting to show and there are women far more attractive and in better shape, but I do try to take care of myself and look nice for him. I've noticed his eye straying a bit when we are out in public and I have always chosen to ignore it. I pretend I don't see. I've asked John what I can do to make things better and he says nothing can make it better. He thinks divorce is the only option and I'm beyond protesting." She pauses. "I don't know how we are going to tell the kids."

"I'm so sorry, Libby," I say, putting my arm around her, my heart aching for her. Libby and John have been married for twenty-five years and have raised four children. They have always seemed so happy. It seems they have just been playing their parts well and it has been an illusion. I am sad for them, but this will surely devastate their family. I continue to listen, offering what comfort I can.

"I thought real love was supposed to be unconditional. I mean we've had trials like everyone else and we've somehow made it through them, but . . . this is the most painful thing I've ever had to deal with. To know he no longer wants me the way I want him just hurts my heart. Why am I not good enough anymore?"

"You are better than good enough. You are an amazing person and you are very beautiful. If he can't see that, then it is his loss."

Libby gives me a watery smile. "Thank you, Giselle."

Before I leave, I hug her and again tell her how great she is, and that her value is beyond price. We women tend to forget that most of the time and need to be reminded.

If I could only make myself believe . . .

During my drive home, I contemplate my own marriage. I am blessed to have Julian, and I have always felt nothing could ever come between us. The day we married was the happiest of my life, and I will forever be grateful for the trip I took with some friends to Scotland on my twentieth birthday. Because it completely changed my life.

Three years ago.

Glasgow, Scotland

Famished after a long day of shopping, we stopped in a pub to grab a quick bite before heading back to the bed and breakfast we were staying at. The place had just started getting busy when this tall, muscular, drop-dead gorgeous man walked up on the small stage with his guitar and started singing. He was amazing! My eyes immediately connected with his and stayed connected for the entire hour. I was glued to my seat. Our food was long gone and my friends had been ready to leave for some time, but their attempts to get me to leave were futile. The Scottish god and I smiled at one another the entire time. It was as if we were the only two people there and he was singing just for me. Little did I know he was the owner of the pub, as well as a few others scattered all over Scotland.

As soon as his set was done, he approached my table. He had looked astounding on stage, but up close he was walking perfection!

He greeted the four of us, but his gaze was still fixed on me. "I'm Julian Mackenzie," he said, introducing himself, and before I could give him my name in return he asked, "Do ye believe in love at first sight, love? Please tell me ye do, darlin', because if ye should get up an' leave, ye will be takin' ma heart with ye."

My friends sighed and giggled like school girls.

"Really?" I said, smiling.

"Oh, aye. I cannae let ye get awa' now. T'would be the death o me, an' ye wouldnae wan' tha' on yer conscience now, would ye?"

"No, I wouldn't want that."

"Then we are in agreement. For the sake o ma health, ye must stay til I can see ye back safely ta where yer goin', and then ye must promise me the opportunity ta win yer heart for ma own."

"Girls, I think that's our cue," my friend, Merrilyn said. "Good to meet you," she gushed, ushering the others away from the table. "See you later, Giselle."

"Giselle, is it?" Julian said, his smile wide. "A bonnie name for a verra bonnie lassie."

My face grew warmer. "Thank you. And you are an ummm . . . bonnie laddie . . . did I say that right?"

"Och, aye. An' I thank ye, Giselle. Now, gettin' back ta ma heart, tis at this verra moment beatin' only for ye, an' if I

donnae make ye mine, ye may as weel bury me because the life will be bleedin' right oot o me."

"So, are you saying I would be saving you life?"

"Aye, tha's the truth o it."

I heave a dramatic sigh. "Well, I guess I should do my part in helping to preserve your life."

He grins. "Aye. I thank ye, fair Giselle." He held a strong hand out to me and I placed mine in it, basking in the warmth of his smile as he closed his fingers around mine.

And that was it for me. My heart was already his and I hadn't even given him my last name. With his lightly-bearded face, brilliant blue eyes, muscular physique, and lush black hair, which was secured in a ponytail, I should have automatically assumed this was a rehearsed come-on, but the intensity of his gaze said it wasn't. We truly claimed one another's hearts that night.

For the rest of my time in Scotland, Julian and I were inseparable. He introduced my friends to some of his male friends and they were occupied for the duration. My days with Julian were wonderful, full of fun, laughter and loving embraces. His kisses were amazingly-decadent and completely addicting, and we couldn't seem to get enough of each other. Being with him had shifted my whole world and made everything fall into place.

Julian was beautiful, funny and talented, and I was frequently a recipient of that talent and his hilarious sense of humor. He would sing Scottish folk songs to me and share funny stories. I loved his voice, whether singing or simply speaking. The gentle cadence of his accent was almost soothing at times.

Every night he performed, I was there, at the same table up front, and his eyes were always on me, which earned me some pretty envious stares, sometimes glares. But I didn't mind. Each night he ended with the same song, and always dedicated it to me.

> My love is like a red red rose
> That's newly sprung in June
> O my love is like a melodie
> Thats sweetly play'd in tune
> As fair art thou, my bonnie lass,
> So deep in love am I
> And I will love thee still, my dear,
> Till a' the seas gang dry.

My dreams were always pleasant.

"Ye ken, I saw a leprechaun once," he told me one night after closing up. He sat down at my table and pulled me onto his lap.

"You did?" I grinned, arching a brow. "You saw a leprechaun, here in Scotland?"

"I did in deed."

"Well, do tell."

He smiled at the unbelieving smirk on my face. "Weel, when I was five years auld, ma faither took me on a picnic. I didnae remember the name o the place, but I do remember it was bonnie. There were green rollin' hills an' the sky was so blue. It looked like a scene from a fairy tale.

"I was sittin' in the grass playin' ma wee guitar when a butterfly flew by. It was verra bonnie. The butterfly flew towards a small row o trees an' I chased it into the grove. When I cam' oot on the other side o the trees, I couldnae find the butterfly. It had disappeared.

"I became verra sad. Since I couldnae find it, I turned ta go back to ma faither when I heard this wee voice. I turned aroun', an' low an' behold, there was a wee leprechaun. He stood lookin' up at me with a big smile on his face."

""Why are ye so sad, child?" he asked me, his big blue eyes a twinklin'.

"I wanted ta play with the butterfly," I said, "But it flew awa'."

"There, there, child," he said, "I'll play with ye." I was so excited. A real live leprechaun wanted ta play with me."

"Tell me yer name, child," he said.

"Julian. Wha's yers?"

"Ma name is Patrick." He took o his cap an' bowed ta me. Then he taught me some games an' we laughed an' played. Pretty soon we sat under one o the trees an' he told me stories. Wonderful, fantastic stories, some o which I ken an' some I didnae. After a while, I started ta yawn. I was tired after runnin' aroun' an' playin' all those games. He took o his wee green jacket an' filled it with shamrocks. Then he placed it on the grass under the tree for me ta use as a pillow. Even though it t'was small, t'was the softest pillow I ha' ever felt. Then he said, "Now child, let me tell ye one last story.""

Julian stopped at that point.

"So what happened?" I asked. He had my curiosity peaked.

"I dinnae know," he said. "The next thin' I ken, ma faither was kneelin' by me under the tree. I ha' fallen asleep there."

"So, it was all a dream," I said, smiling.

"Maybe," he said, a slight smile playing on his lips.

With all the detail with which he told the story, I might have actually believed him, if I hadn't known better. "Well, even if it was a dream, it was a good story."

J. Adams

"Aye. Ye ken, I never eve' told ma faither tha' story."

"Really? Then I feel very special that you shared it with me."

"Ye are *special," he said, kissing me. "The most special person in the world ta me. An' wha' made the experience eve' more special was the fact tha' it happened o St. Patrick's Day." He grinned and winked.*

I chuckled. "Now that's classic."

"Ye cannae tell anyone. If it got oot tha' I was dreamin' o the wee green guy, the Scots would run me oot on a rail."

"All right, I promise not to tell a soul." In return for my promise, he gifted me with a kiss so full of passion, it left me weak. I definitely had sweet dreams that night.

The next day, after spending an hour at Loch Ness, hoping in vain to get a photo of the famous Nessie, Julian took me to see the Sir William Wallace monument. Standing in front of the imposing structure, wrapped in Julian's arms, I was awe-struck.

I relaxed against him. "I wonder what he was really like?"

"Good man an' a great warrior, but complicated. Did ye see Braveheart?"

"Yes, I loved that movie."

"Nice movie, but no completely accurate. Then again, movies seldom are."

"True, but hey, it's Mel Gibson! Seeing that man in a kilt is the stuff of dreams."

"Dreamin' o Mel Gibson, are ye?" he growled against my ear.

"Yeah, but that was before you. I'm sure you look a thousand times better in a kilt."

"A thousand? Ye thin' so?"

"Definitely. But getting back to the movie, you gotta admit the love story about him and his probably-fictitious wife makes good Hollywood romance."

Julian laughed. *"Och, aye. Yer right aboot tha'. Which is why I wanted ta bring ye here . . . ta propose ta ye in front o Scotland's greatest warrior."*

"What?" I whispered, turning around. He knelt and my emotions bubbled to the surface, accompanied by tears.

"I ken I'm no a knight, but I promise ta be as faithful an' honorable as a knight, ta love an' treasure ye with all tha' I am, if ye will be ma wife." He pulled a small box from his pocket and opened it, revealing a ring—a single solitaire surrounded by tiny emeralds and set on a white gold band.

"Will ye marry me, darlin'? I love ye with all ma heart an' I hav' ta make ye mine."

I was so overcome with emotion, I couldn't speak. With tears splashing down my cheeks, I nodded. He smiled and placed the ring on my finger, and then he stood and took me in his arms.

After taking me to Edinburgh to meet his parents and his brother and sister, Julian moved to the states and we were married two months later. We went back to Scotland for our honeymoon and had a traditional Scottish wedding ceremony for his family. I got to see Julian in a wedding kilt twice, and he was definitely a million times sexier than Mel.

Since then, our love for each other has increased with each passing day. Sure, there will always be obstacles to overcome, but we are both determined to do any and everything we can to insure that our love will stay strong enough to withstand anything.

Even hair loss?

My thoughts return to the present as I pull into the driveway. I say a quick prayer for Libby and John before going into the house. Julian is standing at the kitchen counter buttering a piece of bread.

"How was yer visit?"

I walk over to him and wrap my arms around his neck, hugging him tightly.

"Wha's this for?" he asks, his deep voice soft.

"I'm just so happy to be your wife."

His embrace tightens. "An' I'm glad ta be yer husband." He draws back a little, looking into my eyes. "Did somethin' happen?"

I take his hand and we move to the table. While Julian eats, I tell him about Libby and John. The news takes him by surprise as well. Swallowing the last of the bread, he scoots his chair closer to mine. "Ah, darlin', I cannae imagine wha' they must be goin' through."

I nod, heaving a small sigh. "She is hurting so much. I feel sorry for them."

Julian takes my hands in his. "T'will be hard, but they will get through it somehow. Libby is a strong woman an' I'm sure she appreciated havin' ye ta talk to."

I flick a tear away. "Julian, promise me we will always be close. I don't think I could bear it if we weren't."

Pulling me from my chair onto his lap, he wraps me in his warm embrace. "We will, *mo nighean donn*. I promise." He meets my lips with his, kissing me tenderly. "I love ye, Giselle. An' tha' willnae ever change."

"I love you," I murmur against his mouth.

Then, deepening his kiss, he endeavors to prove his words.

Chapter 4

Let there be nothing within thee that is not very beautiful and very gentle, and there will be nothing without thee that is not beautiful and softened by the spell of thy presence.

James Allen

As soon as we get past some major turbulence, I loosen my death grip on Julian's hand. "Sorry," I say as he flexes his fingers.

"Tis all right, darlin'." He gives me a reassuring smile. "I wouldnae give up the use o ma hand for anyone but ye."

"Thanks," I say, leaning over to kiss him. "Is that better?"

"Weel, let me see." he again flexes his fingers. "T'will do for now." I elbow him and he grins, lacing my fingers through his, kissing my hand.

A male flight attendant, making his way down the aisle, stops by our seats with the service cart.

"What would you like, Ma'am?" The young man's grin widens as he leans over Julian to serve me. Julian releases a low snort and I nudge him.

"Can I get you anything else?" he asks, turning on his best southern charm.

"No, thank you," I say, glancing at Julian's amused expression, and then across the aisle at Dad's matching grin where he sits with Aidan.

"Well, if you need anything else, don't hesitate to let me know."

I wait to see if Julian will receive the same syrupy hospitality, and I'm actually kind of surprised when he doesn't. The attendant serves Julian his drink without conversation.

"Now, as I said, if you need anything," he says, putting emphasis on *anything*, "don't hesitate to ask." His eyes never leave mine as he makes this offer, and though I am flattered–especially now when my confidence is so floundering–I almost want to punch him in the eye with my wedding ring. And it is obvious that Julian is thoroughly enjoying this. Once the attendant moves up the aisle, I playfully punch him. "Oh, you!"

"Wha'?" he asks innocently.

"You know what. What's with the grin?"

"Och, I was just admirin' his warm southern hospitality."

"Right."

As we exit the plane and stop for a moment before heading down to baggage claim, the flight attendant who served us comes through the gate.

"This is my stop," he drawls as he casually walks by, winking at me. This time Julian laughs out loud.

"Julian!" I whisper sternly, trying to keep from laughing, myself. "I can't believe you!"

"An' I cannae believe the lad was so bold. Maybe I should go after him an' bend him like a pretzel. Wha' do ye think, Jack?"

Dad laughs. "I would definitely pay to see it."

Dad scoops Mark into a massive hug, almost lifting him off the floor. "It's so good to see you."

"It's good to see you, too."

Dad moves aside so Julian and I can greet Mark. "I'm so glad you could come," he tells us.

"Thanks for invitin' us," Julian says, putting an arm around Mark's shoulder.

"It just wouldn't have been the same without you guys."

Mark walks us over to baggage claim to retrieve our luggage, all the while talking excitedly about the wedding plans. He also tells us about the things he has planned for us to do while we are here.

"I'm so glad you guys could come early."

"Weel, we wanted ta be able ta spend time with ye before the weddin'," Julian says.

"And we can't wait to meet your bride to be," I add.

"I'm looking forward to introducing you. She's pretty awesome."

Mark holds Aidan, keeping him occupied while we keep a lookout for our luggage. Soon we have everything loaded into his mother's minivan and are on our way.

"It's so beautiful here," I say, taking in the massive mountains in the distance, and Julian agrees.

"I can't argue with you there," Mark says. "It's so different from the east, and I never realized just how beautiful it really is or how much I missed it until I came back. It struck me all over again."

"I can understand why," Dad says.

"Tomorrow we'll take you guys out and really show you some sights."

Julian slaps him on the shoulder. "We look forward ta it."

Chapter 5

Every beauty which is seen here below by persons of perception resembles more than anything else that celestial source from which we all are come.

Unknown

"You have a beautiful home," Dad comments as we pull into the driveway and I readily agree.

Theirs is a large home of total southwestern design. From the flat, red tiled roof to the beige stucco, it is lovely.

"Everyone is back in the family room," Mark says. "Just follow the loud laughter."

Julian chuckles. "It does sound like everyone is havin' a good time back there."

"All of my sisters and their families are here. Whenever we get together, it's an automatic party."

Mark leads us into the family room and everyone converges at once, anxious to meet us. Mark quickly makes the introductions.

"Make yourselves comfortable," his mother, Margret says. "Mark has told us so much about you, we feel like you're a part of the family."

"He's told us a lot about all of you, too," I say. "It's a pleasure to finally meet you." Their kindness makes us feel welcome and at home.

"What a cutie," Mark's sister, Afton says, cooing at Aidan. "How old is he?"

"He just turned a year old a couple of weeks ago," I answer.

"He's a little version of his dad," Margret says.

Mark's dad, Rick, holds his hands out to Aidan. "Hi, little guy." Aidan reaches for his hand, then Rick holds his arms open and Aidan jumps right into them. "I think I've made a friend," he says, chuckling.

"Looks like you have," his wife agrees. "Must be those grandpa looks of yours."

"Hey!" he says, pretending to be insulted. "Come on, little guy. Let's go to the playroom and meet the crew." Rick takes Aidan to meet the grandchildren while we all chatter on about the wedding.

"So where is your fiancee," Dad asks."

Mark grins. "She should be here at any time . . . now." The doorbell rings. "That must be her." He runs to answer the door. Ten seconds later he reappears with the love of his life, and introduces us to Sara.

"Isn't she gorgeous?" Mark asks, beaming. It is definitely more of a statement than a question.

"She definitely is," Dad says. "How did you get her?"

Sara laughs. "Well, I got so tired of him scratching at my door, I felt sorry for him and gave in."

The whole room roars with laughter.

"Good one," Mark says, hugging her.

The doorbell rings again.

"I'll get it," Rick says. "That must be Cassie."

"Is she another sister?" I ask.

"No," Mark answers, quickly filling us in. "She was married to our oldest brother that passed away a couple of years ago. She was pregnant at the time, but she lost the baby a few months later."

"How sad," I say, keeping my voice down.

"Yeah, it's was pretty hard on us all. But she is finally doing well."

The grand-kids soon merge in with the adults. Aidan crawls to Dad and tugs on his pant leg. "Uh oh," Dad says, picking him up. "I think someone's sprung a leak."

"Oh, I'm sorry," I tell him. "Let me take him and change him."

"That's okay, I'll do it."

"Are you sure you don't mind?"

"Not at all," he says and I hand him the diaper bag.

Mark offers to show him to one of the guest rooms. "All right, little man, come with Grandpa." Dad calls over his shoulder, "If I'm not back soon, send in the Guard."

Julian laughs and calls back, "No way, yer on yer own."

"You're a lot of help," I say, poking him and he pulls me close."

"Here's our little Spanish beauty," Rick says, entering the family room with a curvy, petite woman.

"I'm sorry I'm so late," she says.

"That's okay, we were just getting started." She hands him a large casserole dish.

"Mmmm, Mark says. "Smells good."

"I got ambitious. I made plum pudding and sauce."

"Now how did you know I've had a craving for your plum pudding?" Mark asks, his voice teasing.

"Oh, I guess it's because every time I come over, you say, "Boy, I sure would love to have some of your plum pudding.'"

Mark chuckles. "I guess you finally got the hint, then."

When she smirks and says "Finally," I snort, instantly liking her. Mark introduces us.

"It's good to meet you," I say, shaking her hand, admiring her exotic features. "You're very beautiful."

"Thank you," she says shyly, tucking a lock of dark hair behind her ear, her Spanish accent thick.

We all migrate to the dining room and Dad returns a moment later. Mark immediately introduces him to Cassie.

I almost gasp as I watch Dad's eyes light up. *No way!* I glance at Julian and he winks at me. *I can't believe it! Finally*!

"It's . . . it's a pleasure to meet you," Dad says, shaking her hand, a wide smile spreading across his face.

"It's good to meet you, too," she says and I watch the two staring at each other.

Wow! I mouth to Julian.

"Well," Rick says, clearing his throat, "shall we have a blessing now?"

I know it is wicked of me, but as Rick blesses the food, I discreetly open my eyes and glance from Dad to Cassie, smiling as I observe them doing the very same thing.

The table is set buffet style, and after we fill our plates, we head out onto the patio where tables are set up for everyone to dine. Most of the family walk around with their plates and talk, but I decide it will be easier to sit and feed Aidan. I spot Cassie sitting alone and head to her table.

"Mind if I join you?"

She smiles. "Not at all. I would love some company."

I pull out a chair and get Aidan situated.

"He's so adorable," she says. "And he looks just like your husband."

"Thank you. And my husband thanks you. He's a handful, and definitely his father's son. "

"I'll bet. You are very fortunate."

"I am," I agree. Taking in her somber expression, I find myself wishing I could read her mind because she seems so reserved. But then again, the hurt of loss runs deep, and though I don't know what it is like to lose a husband and a child, I can greatly empathize.

We talk for a while and discover we have many things in common. We love old movies, reading, traveling, and we possess a terrible dislike for sewing.

"I made a shirt during my senior year in home economics class," Cassie says. "It turned out two sizes too small and I ended up giving it to a friend."

I laugh. "Well, at least your friend got a free shirt out of it. I'm sure she was happy."

"Oh she was. She told me to feel free to keep sewing and she would just sit back and patiently wait for me to furnish her new wardrobe."

"That sounds like a plan."

"Well, fortunately, my teacher took pity on me and let me do other domestic things."

"Good teacher."

"Yeah, I haven't touched a sewing machine since."

During a lull in the conversation, I turn and scan the yard for Julian. Instead, I find Dad intently staring at Cassie. He smiles at her and she smiles back.

Oh, this is just too good!

"Mark told me how hard it was on your father to lose your mother."

"It was. He left for work that morning, then came home to find her lying on the floor having had a heart attack. She

47

was already gone." I swallow hard against the swell of emotion I still feel at the memory. "It has taken him a while, but emotionally, he's in a good place now."

"I understand." She quickly looks his way again. "He's very handsome."

Glancing at Dad, I mentally agree. He is a very attractive man. From his short, tousled, slightly-graying blond hair, to his amazing dimples and the small cleft in his chin, to his beautiful pale gray eyes. *He's definitely a good looking guy.* Dad has always kept himself in shape and he is almost as lean and muscular as Julian.

As I watch the object of our conversation approach our table, Aidan reaches up and tangles his fingers in my hair. When I pull his hand away, a generous amount of my hair is in his fist. My heart lurching from both shock and sadness, I quickly leave to give Cassie and Dad some privacy to get to know each other.

And to get rid of the hair.

Instead of going back outside, I change Aidan into his pajamas and sit in the comfortable rocker in our room, quietly holding him. He is so tired, he can hardly keep his eyes open, and I know in another minute he will be asleep. I hold his little hand in mine, pulling a stray strand of my hair from between his fingers. The laughter of the Hayes' grandchildren softly filters through the cracked window and I smile, grateful for our own little boy. He brings so much love and laughter to our life and makes my heart lighter. I really need that now.

I frequently tell myself I should be ashamed that I haven't been handling the hair issue better, because there are so many people in the world with trials a million times greater than mine. Still, that fact doesn't make this any easier, but at the moment it strengthens my resolve to be more positive.

I look up as Julian sticks his head through the half-opened door.

"Are ye all right, love?" he whispers.

I nod and smile. "I'm fine, just a little tired."

"I didnae mean ta abandon ye oot there."

"You didn't abandon me, you were socializing. I'm glad you were able to get to know Mark's family. They are great people. And I enjoyed talking with Cassie. She and dad are really hitting it off."

"Aye, they seem ta be gettin' on weel enough."

I stand and place Aiden in the portable play yard Mark's sister was kind enough to lend us. Tucking the blanket around him, I watch him sleep for a moment. I can feel Julian's gaze and I try to brighten my countenance without much success. Julian slips his arms around me and it takes all my strength to keep from giving in to my urge to have a good cry. There would be no way I could blame that on being tired.

He kisses my ear. "Are ye sure yer all right?"

I lean back against him, longing to melt into him, and his arms tighten around me. "I'm fine."

"Would ye like me ta sit an' hold ye a bit?"

"I would."

We move over to the small sofa by the window. Wrapped in his arms, I close my eyes against the tears and rest my head against his chest. I love that he is so perceptive to my needs. He simply holds me in silence.

"I love you, Julian," I whisper, feeling myself starting to drift off, the combination of the trip and the emotional strain taking a toll on me. I am sure a good night's sleep is just what I need.

His lips caress my brow. "I love ye, *mo nighean donn.*"

Julian

Something has been bothering Giselle for a while now. He can see it in her eyes at times, feel it in her embrace. He wishes he could read her mind, see inside her heart. He longs to take whatever is troubling her and throw it away, to heal whatever is hurting with his love.

Giselle has always been the most open and giving person he has ever known, always concerned for others and putting everyone else first. She is completely devoted to him and their son, and he can't imagine a better wife, nor can he imagine ever being without her.

Julian's thoughts stray to John and Libby and their failing marriage. To have a marriage fall apart after twenty-five long years together is a sadness he can't possibly comprehend. After being together so long, there shouldn't be anything a couple can't overcome. However, he will not judge. He can only keep Libby and John in his prayers and hope that one way or another, all will be well with them.

Softly rummaging his lips over Giselle's brow, he closes his eyes, again wishing to know what is wrong and how he can help.

Help me ta know, God. Help me ta know wha' tis' in her heart an' how I can help. If she has need o me, I wan' ta be there for her. I need ta be there for her. She is everythin' ta me.

He holds her tighter.

Help me ta be wha' she needs.

Chapter 6

Truth exists for the wise, beauty for the feeling heart.

Friedrich Schiller

"She is amazing!" Dad tells us the next morning.

Julian and I exchange knowing smiles. "How late were ye oot with the lassie last night?"

"Oh . . . until after midnight."

I whistle, shooting him a wide grin. "She's a special lady, Dad. And it's obvious to everyone she is as taken with you as you are with her."

"She *is* something special," Dad agrees. "But what about the age difference? I mean, I know there is ten years between you two, but there is twelve between us. You think it makes a difference?"

"No, Jack," Julian answers. "In fact, I thin' I read in one o those magazines for women tha' the lassies are beginnin' ta like older men. Isna tha' right, darlin'?"

"Hmmm, and just when did you start reading these magazines?"

"Weel, when we get the new shipments in at the store, sometimes I cannae help pickin' up one every now an' then ta see wha' new thins' we men need ta learn ta keep up with ye females."

Dad laughs and I snort. "An' just wha' new thins' hav' ye learned, ma husband?"

"Nothin' new, just the same auld thins' we already know. I guess we're so daft, thins' just need ta be repeated. Maybe one day wee'll get it right, eh?"

I smile sweetly, continuing my imitation of his Scottish brogue. "I thin' ye just did, love."

Julian smiles and kisses me. "Anywa', Jack, the age thing means nothin'. I thin' ye should just go for it. Go where the heart leads ye." He smiles, caressing my face. "The heart t'will never lead ye astra'."

I return my beloved husband's smile, pressing my hand to his face. "I agree completely." Staring into one another's eyes for a long moment, we speak everything that is in our hearts.

Dad clears his throat and smiles. "All right, I will, then. Thank you both."

Chapter 7

The best part of beauty is that which no picture can express.

Francis Bacon

Mark and Sara's wedding is held at a reception hall owned by a family friend and is absolutely beautiful. Red and white floral decorations lit up by strands of clear Christmas lights adorn the entire hall. There is a live band playing during the reception, and even from where I stand in the kitchen, they sound great.

A moment later, a familiar voice takes me by complete surprise. I dash into the dance hall and hurry to the front, gasping in happiness as I meet Julian's sensual grin. It seems Mark and Sarah had asked him to perform with the band and he hadn't told me. My sexy husband is singing solo and playing a borrowed guitar! His tie is loosened, and his white tux jacket and vest are off, leaving him wearing only the white shirt and black slacks. Both fit his muscular body like a glove. I watch the women and teenage girls around me swoon as he sings one of my favorite Scottish folk songs.

I love a lassie, a bonnie Hielan' lassie,

If ye saw her ye would fancy her as well.

I met her In September, popp'd the question in November,

So I'll soon be havin' her a' to masel'!

Her faither has consented, so I'm feelin' quite contented

Cause I've been and sealed the bargain wi' a kiss.

I sit and weary, weary, when I think aboot ma deary,

An' you'll always hear me singing this:

He winks at me and I blow him a kiss as he sings the chorus.

'I love a lassie, a bonnie, bonnie lassie,

She's as pure as the lily in the dell,

She's as sweet as the heather, The bonnie bloomin'
heather,

Giselle, ma Scotch Bluebell.'

How I love it when he does that with a song! It's his way of letting everyone know his heart is completely taken.

Julian sings to me frequently and I never tire of hearing his deep, soulful voice, especially when he is singing a romantic Scottish tune, but having him look at me this way in the crowded reception hall is nearly my undoing, and I fight the urge to yank him off the stage, then drag him into one of the back rooms for some serious loving. His grin widens, and I know *he* knows what I am thinking. Before he reaches the chorus again, he mouths, *Later, darlin'*, and my face grows warm.

Once the reception is over and Mark and Sara leave for their honeymoon, Julian and I decide to take a little tour of the bed and breakfast next to the reception center before leaving. The old Victorian home is for sale and owned by the same family friend. We both fall in love with the place the moment we walk in. There is cherry wood trim and molding throughout the house, and all the flooring is hardwood. It has ten large bedrooms, each with a private bath, as well as a large formal living and dining room, and a huge kitchen, fully equipped with every modern convenience.

"It's beautiful," I say. "I really love it, but I think I love our home more. There's just something about the plantation style that I have always favored."

"Me, too. *Our* home really feels like home." Wrapping his arms around me, he presses his nose against the curve of my neck. "An' speakin' o home, I cannae wait ta get ye back an' make mad passionate love ta ye in our own room."

"I'm looking forward to that, too," I breathe, soaking in the warmth of his body against mine. "After that performance today, I long for that more than I can say."

"Weel, shall we go back an' pack then, love?" His voice is husky and full of longing.

"I'll race you to the car."

Julian and I are walking through a Scottish meadow. The grass is the perfect shade of green and wildflowers dot the countryside, their colors vivid and crisp. My hand is tucked in his as we walk and we are talking, but he never looks at me, he just stares straight ahead.

We end up at the crest of a large hill. A crowd of people suddenly appears and Julian smiles, pulling me onward.

"Julian, look at me. Why won't you look at me?"

He doesn't answer. When we are a few yards away from the crowd, a strong gust of wind surges forth, lifting my hair. Then my long locks begin to peel away from my scalp and float upward with the breeze. The crowd begins to laugh and I touch my head, gasping to find all of my hair gone and I'm completely bald. Julian finally turns to me and smiles, before throwing his head back and laughing loudly.

"This is why I willnae look at ye, Giselle. Wha' man could stand ta look at someone so repulsive."

"You can't mean that, Julian. You can't."

"I can an' I do."

As the tears begin to trickle down my cheeks he laughs even harder. I again try to speak, but no words come forth and I am struck mute. Then a beautiful blond takes Julian's hand. He pulls her close and kisses her passionately, burying his fingers in her thick hair. When they part, he takes her hand and they walk away.

"Julian, please! You can't leave me! Please don't leave me?" I silently scream his name until he and the blond are but a dot in the distance. I drop to my knees and sob.

I awaken, moaning, my face wet with tears.

"Giselle, darlin', are ye all right?" I can't answer. "Giselle?" I try to turn away from him, but he stops me. "Wha' is it?"

"It was just a dream," I finally manage.

"Com' here, darlin'." He draws me to him and I bury my face in his chest. "Tis' all right, angel. It wasnae real."

It was real to me. He kisses my brow and continues to hold me close. I desperately cling to him like a woman drowning in the sea, and try to calm my emotions. After a long while, I finally drift off.

Chapter 8

Beauty is not caused. It is.

Emily Dickinson

Dad informs us that he is planning to stay a while longer and spend more time with Cassie, and I couldn't be happier. She is an amazing lady, and after getting to know her more, I can't imagine a better person for Dad. He is happier than I have seen him since Mama passed away. Watching the two of them over the past week, I have seen their affection for one another grow, and I'm keeping my fingers crossed that things will continue to go well.

When Dad comes back two weeks later, it is with ecstatic news. He and Cassie are engaged. I tearfully hug him as he shares with us how much they love each other. He hadn't ever thought he would feel this way again about another woman. I remind him that God has a plan for each of us. We simply need to open our hearts and let it happen.

He shares his decision to put one of his employees in charge of his architect business and settle in Utah. They have even found a home and it turns out to be the Victorian home we walked through after Mark and Sara's reception. They want to have a few kids to help fill the place. The thought of him being so far away and no longer seeing him as much makes me sad, but I could never begrudge them the happiness they deserve.

Dad also tells me he would like to take me away for a week for some father-daughter time. While I am excited to go–he won't tell me where–I have never been away from Julian and Aidan for more than a day. Julian assures me they will be okay, and says though he will miss me to distraction, I need to spend this time with Dad since he will be marrying soon and moving away.

Dad has me wait with Julian while he checks our luggage and picks up our tickets. He is still keeping our destination a secret for as long as he can. I cuddle Aidan, noting the smile on Julian's face.

"You know where he's taking me, don't you?"

His smile widens, his pride in being able to keep the secret so long apparent. I give him an impatient smirk and he laughs.

"I can't believe you, keeping secrets from your own wife," I say, pretending to be hurt.

"Och, swee'heart, I wouldnae keep secrets from ye, just *a* secret." I give him my best pleading look and he averts his eyes. "Come on, darlin', giv' me a break. Yer da made me promise."

"But Julian . . ."

He silences me with a warm kiss. "Yer goin' ta find oot soon enough. He doesnae wan' ye ta know til ye are ready ta go through security an' I gave him ma word I wouldnae tell ye. No matter how guilty ye made me feel." A minute later Dad returns, carrying the tickets and Julian heaves a sigh of relief.

"I see I'm just in time," Dad says, chuckling.

"Aye. Yer daughter was wearin' me down."

"I would never do that," I innocently protest.

"Wha'ever ye say, love."

We walk to the security entrance and Julian draws me into his arms. "I'm goin' ta miss ye, *mo nighean donn*," he whispers against my ear.

"I will miss you, too."

Before getting in line, Dad hands me my ticket and I gasped. "New York! Really?" I have always wanted to go to New York. I jump into his arms and he laughs.

"I knew you would be pleased."

I kiss Aidan's cheek and hold him close another moment. "I'm going to miss you, little guy. You be good for Daddy, okay?"

Julian pulls me close, kissing me tenderly. "I'll miss ye, angel," he breathes into my hair.

"You too," I say again, caressing his cheek.

"Hav' a good time. An' donnae worry aboot anythin'."

"Okay," I sigh. "I'll call you as soon as we get settled."

I wave one last time on the other side of the security area before heading to our gate.

Chapter 9

A thing of beauty is a joy for ever: Its loveliness increases; it will never pass into nothingness; but still will keep a bower quiet for us, and a sleep full of sweet dreams, and health, and quiet breathing...

John Keats

Dad booked a suite for us at the Waldorf Hotel. Just the sight of the building leaves me in awe.

"Wow!" I whisper as we enter the elegant suite. "This is beautiful, Dad."

"I'm glad you like it. I wanted everything to be special."

"It is," I say, hugging him. "Thank you."

"You're welcome. But there are still many surprises to come."

"I'm sure there are, Mr. Big Spender."

He smiles at my use of Mama's pet name for him. "Well, when it comes to spoiling spouses, from what I've seen, your husband could give me a good run."

"True, true."

We take a few minutes to unpack. When I am finished, I call Julian.

"Hi, I made it."

"How was yer flight?"

"It was good. How's Aidan?"

"Och, he cried a wee bit, but he will be okay."

"How are you?" I ask, wishing he were here with me.

"I'm missin' ye, darlin', but I'm all right. Just hav' a good time. Aidan an' I are goin' ta do some male bondin'. T'will be fun."

"Okay, but no wild parties, all right? I wouldn't want the neighbors calling the cops or anything."

"Weel, tis' no fun if we cannae make a wee disturbance, but I promise ta keep Aidan from servin' any jail time, all right?"

"All right," I agree, laughing. "Will you tell him I love him?"

"Already don', darlin'."

"I love you, Julian."

"I love ye, too, an' I'll be thinkin' o you, alwa's."

"Me, too."

I'm just returning to the main sitting area of the suite when there is a knock at the door.

"I'll get it," Dad says with a smile.

"Sir, your limo is ready."

"Thank you. We will be right down."

"Dad, a limo?"

"Yes, a limo."

"I can't believe you did this!" I hug him, kissing his cheek.

"Believe it. While we are here, we are going to travel in style."

"Where are we going?"

"Well, first we are going out to dinner. Then we'll go for a drive around the city and see some of the sights before it gets dark."

I glance down at myself. "Maybe I should change . . ."

"No need. You look great."

We dine at an Italian restaurant and I can't remember eating a better Italian meal. I love everything, from the main dish of stuffed Chicken Marsala to the rich Tiramisu I have for dessert. In fact, the dessert is so good, I order an extra one to go.

"Dinner was great, Dad. Thank you."

"You're welcome. I am glad we could do this. There won't be many opportunities like this after I'm married."

"I know. And I won't allow myself to be sad thinking of you being over a thousand miles away."

His smile is somber. "I'll try not to be sad, too." He pauses, silently looking at me for a moment.

"What is it?"

"You look so much like your mother. You have her beautiful smile and her soft spoken manner." He kisses my hand. "You mean the world to me, and I don't know how I would have made it through this last few years if you hadn't been here for me. I love you so much."

"I love you, too, Dad. And repeating what you what you told me, you are much stronger than you think you are."

"But a large part of that strength comes from you. I have been so blessed to have you as a daughter."

I struggle to keep the tears at bay. "I have been blessed to have you, too."

"I want you to know that even though my life is changing, I will always be here for you."

"Thank you." I smile, not trusting myself to say more for fear that I will start crying and not be able to stop. I will miss my dad more than I can say.

A few minutes later, our waiter is back with my boxed dessert and the check. Dad pays him and thanks him for his great service. Then we leave.

We spend an hour driving around the city, just talking and enjoying our time together.

"So did you and Cassie decide where you are going on your honeymoon?"

"Yes, we have. She has always wanted to go to Europe, so we're going to travel and see the whole country."

"That's so exciting! How long will you be gone?"

"About a month. We want to take our time."

"Be sure to take lots of pictures."

"We will. Cassie is very much into scrap booking, so I'm sure we will be bringing back a suitcase full of photos."

By the time we make it back to the hotel, it is 11:00 and we're both pretty tired. I place my packages on the sofa and hug Dad. "Thank you for a wonderful day."

"You're welcome. Now go and get some sleep. We have a big day tomorrow."

"Bigger than today? Is that possible?"

"Just wait and see."

"Okay, since I have no choice." He chuckles and kisses my brow. "Goodnight, Dad."

"Goodnight, honey."

Chapter 10

The most beautiful things in the world cannot be seen or even touched, they must be felt with the heart.

Helen Keller

Julian

Having finished his breakfast, Julian smiles as he watches his son eat his soggy toast, dripping with the milk he'd dumped on it. "Tha's definitely an acquired taste," he says, clearing off the table.

As he fills the dishwasher, Julian's thoughts wander to Giselle. It has only been a day, but he misses her immensely.

The only time they have ever been apart is the one day each year that she spends with her father. The two have always been close and Julian can tell she is more heartbroken about the move than she is letting on. But Giselle is strong that way, the strongest woman he has ever known, and he loves her to distraction. Being without her for a whole week is going to be tough. But she and her dad need this time.

We will have plenty of time to make up. The thought makes him smile and warmth spreads through him.

Giselle is everything to him, the light of his life, the very air he breathes, and her very essence keeps him steady. Even now, knowing she is in New York with her father, he subconsciously wanders through the house looking for her, feeling a part of him missing. It's as if his heart is driven to seek her out. The final verse of her favorite Scottish song comes to mind.

> *Tho' 'twere ten thousand mile, my love*
> *Tho' t'were ten thousand mile,*
> *And I will come again my love,*
> *Tho' t'were ten thousand mile.*

Julian could never have guessed when he went to work that night at his pub in Glasgow that his entire life was about to change. The moment he walked up on the small stage with his guitar, then turned around and looked into her eyes, she captured his heart and soul, and he had felt driven to make her his. Never in his life had anything like that ever happened to him. He hadn't dated anyone in over a year, and it hadn't been because of lack of opportunity. The way women threw themselves at him regularly had been both nauseating and off-putting. But Giselle had been different. He *felt* different just being near her. He knew she would most likely think he was using a line to pick her up, but somehow his heart had spoken to hers, and he knew if she hadn't been open to him and the words he spoke–words that hadn't come to him until the moment he approached her table–he would have been lost. She possessed complete power over him and she hadn't even known it.

Drawing his thoughts back to the present, Julian turns as Aidan holds out his plate, and he quickly takes it before the little boy becomes impatient and drops it.

"All don', laddie?" He cleans his son up and takes him up to the playroom. Then he heads back down to finish cleaning the kitchen, missing the finishing touch Giselle normally adds. He is wiping off the counter when the phone rings.

"Hello."

"Hi, it's me."

"Hi, me," he says, happy to talk to her.

"How are things this morning?"

"All right, darlin', except I'm missin' ye somethin' fierce."

"I miss you so much. I just woke up and thoughts of you have been swimming in my head."

He grins, imagining her dreamy smile. "Great minds thin' alike." He wishes he could be there beside her, holding her warmth against him.

"How is Aidan this morning?"

"He's fine. He just finished eatin' breakfast with its usual sogginess."

Giselle laughs. "He always has to apply the finishing touch on his meal before he even gets started."

"He definitely does." Julian leans back against the wall and closes his eyes, enjoying the sound of her voice. "How was yer night?"

"It was wonderful. Dad had a limo pick us up and take us to dinner. Then we took a drive around the city."

"A limo, huh?" Tell the auld man tha's goin' ta be a hard act ta follow. Does tha' mean I should hav' one waitin' at the airport when ye return?"

"No, thank you. I would much rather ride up front next to you. Besides, what would I do with my back seat drivers license?"

Julian grins. "We definitely cannae let tha' go ta waste. So, wha' are ye doin' today?"

"I don't know. Dad wouldn't tell me. I guess I am in for another surprise . . . unless you know something. Do you?"

"No, darlin'. But even if I did, I wouldnae tell ye."

"Thanks a lot."

"Sure." He chuckles softly. "You hav' a good day today an' donnae worry aboot anythin', all right?"

"You have a good day, too. I'll be thinking about you."

"And I ye. I love ye more than anythin', Giselle."

"I love you too."

After hanging up, I lay in bed a minute longer and speculate about today's activities. I know it is pointless to ask Dad what he has planned, so I decide to just go with it and let myself be excited about being surprised. I also decide a relaxing bubble bath would be a great way to start the morning. I can't remember the last time I indulged myself with a long soak.

I finally get up and head to the closet to pick out an outfit for the day. *It would help if I knew what we were doing.* I quickly put the question out of my mind and settle on a knee-length white floral skirt, a red crochet top with a matching cardigan, and gold gladiator sandals. This is an outfit for anything.

Heading to the bathroom, I place my clothes on the bed and freeze. Hesitantly, I approach the head of the bed, shocked to see a lock of my hair lying on the pillow. I reach up and bury my fingers in the thick tresses, startled to feel a large bare spot on the back of my scalp.

No, no. This can't be happening!

Hurrying into the bathroom, I grab a hand mirror from the vanity and turn to examine the back of my head. There is no need to separate the hair. The two-inch wide bald spot is hard to miss. Sitting on the edge of the tub, I drop my face in my hands, tears slipping through my fingers.

My hair has been continually thinning a little each day, but this . . . I never expected it to get this bad. I am really losing my hair. I'm losing the thick tresses Julian loves so much. I have had long hair all my life and have never had it cut, not even a trim. Never!

Just a couple of days ago, I finally broke down and searched the internet, researching hair loss. Alopecia. Or in my case, severe Alopecia Areata. I found a list of things a doctor can prescribe, but they may not work.

Taking a deep breath, I mentally review what I found.

In the worst cases the condition progresses (gradually or quickly) until large areas of hair have been lost. These cases naturally bring distress to the people affected. When the condition first appears, it is not possible to predict whether it will be mild and recover soon or become severe. Apart from the uncommon type which is accompanied by eczema in children, no information is available about this. Everyone hopes that early treatment will stop the progress of the condition but if the alopecia is destined to be severe, this course may still be followed despite treatment.

Every link I followed said the same thing.

I'm losing my hair. What will Julian think? Reaching up, I comb my fingers through it, releasing a soft sob as more comes out in my hand. Wiping my face, I grab a couple of hair combs and some Bobbie pins and style my hair in a loose up-do, turning my head one way, and then another, making sure the bald spot is concealed. Having been pretty much satisfied with my looks for most of my life, right now my emotions are thrown out of whack and I suddenly feel like an ugly duckling.

I turn the water on and pour in some fragrant bubble bath, compliments of the hotel. Rinsing away the rest of my tears, I undress and get in the tub. A few minutes later, I absently turn the water off and sit back, staring off into space, and try to calm my thoughts.

Like it will make a difference.

Chapter 11

Beauty is not in the face; beauty is a light in the heart.

Kahlil Gibran

Dad surprises me with a day of shopping in Manhattan. He takes me up and down Fifth Avenue, making sure we enter almost every store. I am speechless with each purchase he makes for me. In one store, I try on evening gowns. Normally, they would make me feel elegant, but not today. When I tell Dad can't decide between three of them, he buys them all, making sure I pick out shoes to match. Our last stop is Tiffany's, where he buys me a beautiful pair of diamond earrings.

"Dad, you're spoiling me," I say with false cheerfulness as we get back in the limo.

"I know, and I love spoiling my daughter."

"Where exactly are you planning to take me?"

"You'll see."

Later, I change into a dark green velvet gown, adding the diamond earrings. Normally, I would wear my hair down with something so dressy, but I can't. I should feel beautiful, but all I can think about is the large concealed bald spot. I give myself another look over, then go out to the main room to wait for Dad. A moment later, he comes out of his room and whistles.

"Oh, Giselle! If Julian could only see you right now! You are beautiful."

"Thank you, Dad. You're very handsome, yourself."

"Thank you." He is wearing a classic black tuxedo with a dark green bow tie. I silently admire him, thinking what a lucky woman Cassie is.

"Are you ready?" he asks taking my hand.

"Yes." I have been looking forward to this evening and I am going to do my best to leave my worries at the hotel.

Dad takes me to dinner, and then to the Metropolitan Opera to see *The Phantom of the Opera,* and though I am enjoying the play, a small part of me feels as ugly and lost as the Phantom and I empathize with the character.

"Are you all right?" Dad asks me on the way back to the hotel.

I smile. "Yes, I'm just a little tired." It isn't a lie really. I *am* tired. Tired of trying not to think about the missing hair and the bare patch of skin, a patch that seems to be growing more with each passing minute. I can no longer ignore it, and I suddenly want to be home with Julian, wrapped in his arms. I need to know my hair loss doesn't matter, that his love for me is unconditional. I look at Dad, unable to hold the tears back any longer.

"Giselle, honey, what's wrong?"

I swallow hard. "Dad, for the past little while, I have been slowly losing my hair, and this morning . . . I found a large clump of hair on my pillow. And it's getting worse."

"Oh, honey, I'm so sorry." His eyes move to my hair. "There has to be something you can do to stop it."

"I researched it. It's a condition called Alopecia. There are things a doctor can prescribe, but mine is severe, and in most cases it progressively gets worse." I pause, tears spilling down my cheeks. "Oh, Dad, I'm so afraid of what Julian will think. He has always loved my hair. I'm sure if he had known in Scotland that the woman he intended to marry would eventually lose all of her hair, he probably would have had second thoughts about the decision." Shaking my head, I wipe my eyes. "I just don't know what to do."

"Giselle, Julian loves you more than life itself and this is not going to matter to him. He didn't fall in love with you because of your hair. He loves *you*, and that will never change."

"I know. At least I hope so. I'm just so worried, not only about what *he* will think, but everyone else, too."

"No one else matters. I promise you, honey, it will be okay."

"I'm sorry, Dad, and I don't mean to sound like a child, but I just want to go home. I really need Julian right now."

"I understand, and don't be sorry. We've had a wonderful time together."

When we reach the hotel, Dad calls the airport and changes our return flight to tomorrow morning. When he is done, he sits next to me and takes my hand.

"Dad." My voice breaks. "Would you hold me?"

"You don't even have to ask." I close my eyes, finding comfort in my father's embrace. After a while, I slowly begin to relax and soon feel myself drifting off.

"I guess I should go to bed now. I'm going to try and get in to see a doctor tomorrow. Slim chance getting an appointment so soon, I know. But I have to do something."

"I hope you can. Goodnight, honey." He kisses my forehead.

"Goodnight, Dad. And thank you."

When I awaken the next morning, the bald spot has grown and another has joined it, and I cry as I collect the hair from my pillow. *It's happening so fast, God. How can it be happening so fast?*

I call a dermatologist, elated that I can get in. I can't get back fast enough.

I spend the entire flight home, praying Julian will understand and be there for me. If nothing works to stop my hair from falling out, I hope he can live with it.

Because I don't know if I can. And I don't know what I will do if he can't.

J. Adams

Chapter 12

The beauty seen, is partly in him who sees it.

Christian Nevell Bovee

$\mathcal{I}$ am grateful Julian isn't home when I arrive because it gives me more time to think about my situation. Dad had taken me straight from the airport to my appointment. The doctor called in a couple of prescriptions for me and I picked them up right after the appointment. He told me my case was so severe, the creams may not work, but I'm trying to be positive. I can't allow myself to do anything less.

When I get back, I unpack and put my things away, as well as the things I bought for Julian and Aidan while I waited for him. His briefcase is gone so he must be at the bookstore. I take a moment to admire the beautiful gowns before hanging them up and smile as I think of Dad and how happy he was to buy them for me. Cassie will definitely be lavished and pampered by her new husband.

I am glad I had the chance to spend that time with Dad, and I wish we hadn't had to cut our trip so short. Before dropping me off, he had stood for a moment holding me and assuring me things will be all right.

Having finished putting everything away, I go down to the kitchen to make myself a cup of chamomile tea, hoping it will help me relax. But anxiousness continues to press at my insides. Here I am, a twenty-three-year-old woman, having to contemplate losing my hair. Heaving a sorrowful sigh, I press my head in my hands and will the tears to stay away. I don't want Julian to see me with red eyes because it would make things worse. How, I don't know.

I jump at the sound of the front door opening. Julian is whistling as he walks down the hallway. The familiar sound brings those dreaded tears to my eyes. I stand and try to smile as he enters the kitchen.

"Giselle! Hey! Wha' are ye . . ."

The moment the first tear slips down my cheek, a torrent follows and in a flash, I am in his arms, my face pressed against his warm chest.

"Wha' is it, darlin'?"

I am unable to answer as heart-wrenching sobs tear through me.

"Shhh, tis' all right, honey."

"Keep holding me, Julian. Please."

Julian scoops me up in his arms and carries me to the living room. He sits down on the sofa and cradles me on his lap. He holds me in silence, but I can feel his heart pounding madly. I finally draw back a little and look into his blue eyes.

"Talk ta me, darlin'. Ye hav' got me scared."

"I'm sorry."

He wipes my tears with gentle hands as his own eyes fill. "Tell me, honey."

How? There are no words I can say that will make this any easier. All I can do is show him. I slowly pull the pins from my hair, and as I do, another small lock of hair falls out.

Julian's eyes widen. "Oh, Giselle! Oh, honey!"

"It started months ago, but the past couple of days . . . Oh, Julian, I'm so sorry." I try to look away, but he catches my chin, forcing me to meet his tear-filled gaze.

"Why are ye sorry? Ye hav' nothin' ta apologize for."

"But I know how much you love . . ."

"I love *ye*," he says, cutting off my words. "I love *ye* an' everythin' aboot ye. Do ye thin' tha' will change because o this?" He lightly caresses the bare spot that is now visible on the front of my scalp. "Tis' no yer hair tha' makes ye beautiful, darlin'. I fell in love with ye for who ye are. I love ye with every fiber o ma bein', and ma love only grows with each day tha' passes."

"But . . . how can you say that? I'm losing it all. By the end of the week, at this rate, it will all be gone. I saw a doctor and he gave me some things to try, but . . . I don't think they will work. How will you be able to look at me? I can barely look at my reflection now." I pause, my lips trembling. "Julian, I don't want you to be ashamed or embarrassed to be seen with me. I can buy a wig and . . . He presses a finger to my lips.

"Listen ta me, darlin'. Yer hair doesnae make ye beautiful. Aye, I hav' alwa's loved it, but losing it doesnae diminish yer beauty, no even a wee bit. Tis ye tha' I love."

I lower my eyes and he again catches my chin in his hand, and I am startled by the tears trailing down his face. "Ah, angel, this is wha' ha' been botherin' ye. Ye hav' held it in for all this time. Why did ye no tell me?"

"I was afraid," I whisper.

"Ah, Giselle, my heart is achin' for ye, for feelin' like ye ha' ta handle this alone. I'm so sorry, love."

"No, *I'm* sorry. You shouldn't have to deal with this."

Julian shakes his head, pulling me close, and draws my head down to his chest. My ear picks up the strong beat of his heart.

"Do ye hear tha', love?" His voice is soft. "Hear how ma heart beats for ye, Giselle. Only for ye. Yer ma heart, ma verra soul. Never doubt ma love for ye, angel. Trust in it. In us. In me." He tilts my face up and lowers his lips to mine. "Never doubt," he whispers before deepening his kiss.

Within seconds, I am on fire. His mouth passionately coaxes and devours mine with heated affection, sending molten lava through my entire body. His tongue dances over mine and I completely melt. Then his mouth is everywhere, branding me, his strong arms and body claiming me. As my tears flow, his love flows into me, soothing the hurt and taking it away. He is my knight, my protection from harm, the holder of my honor, and defender of my heart. In his arms, nothing can touch me. He is all that exists.

"Where is Aidan?" I whisper against his ear, kissing every inch of it.

"With yer grandmother," he breathes, slipping my shirt off my shoulder and covering the area with kisses. "Now, I'm goin' ta take ye upstairs, ma bonnie wife, an' make extremely passionate love ta ye. Is that all right?"

"Aye . . ."

A long while later, Julian gazes down at me, his eyes caressing my face, and the love in them is so clear, it's almost blinding. He kisses me, then lightly rests his forehead against mine.

"Ye are the verra air I breathe, *mo nighean donn.* I cannae imagine no havin' ye in ma life. Ye own ma heart. I am completely yers, as ye are mine. Tha' willnae change, no matter wha'."

Caressing his smooth back, I smile, taking heart in his words, because I know they aren't just words. "I love you."

"An' I love ye." He caresses my face with the back of his hand, his breath fanning my lips as he kisses me, his warm mouth lightly toying with mine. "Someone once said, *'Ye donnae love a woman because she is beautiful, but she is beautiful because ye love her.'* An' they were right. Ye will alwa's be beautiful ta me, Giselle–the most bonnie lass ta ever grace this whole earth."

"Thank you, Julian, for loving me."

"No need ta thank me, darlin'. I wa' born ta love ye."

No other words are spoken because none are needed. And as the passion between us is renewed, it speaks more that can ever be said.

"Do you ever miss it?" I ask later in the night. "Living in Scotland, I mean. Do you ever miss it?"

"Aye," he sighs. "Sometimes. But I am happy here because I am with ye."

I nod. "I miss going to the pub and hearing you sing. I know you sing to me still, but I do miss it sometimes."

"We made a lot o memories there, tha's for sure."

I rise up, resting my chin on his chest, finding his eyes in the dim light of the moon. "What would you think about moving back for a while?" I watch his eyes widen.

"But this is yer home. Ye would really leave?"

I've been giving this some thought for some time now and my answer comes easy. "Dad has a new life now, so nothing is holding me back. I want Aidan, as well as our future children to know their heritage on both sides. It would be fun to go back for a while. We still have the house there. Besides, anywhere we are together is home."

He smiles, his expression one of contemplation. "Aye. T'would be nice ta live in the auld house again, but this time with ye an' Aidan." He caresses my face. "Are ye sure, love?"

"I am."

"All right, then. Home to Scotland it is."

Chapter 13

When you reach the heart of life you shall find beauty in all things, even in the eyes that are blind to beauty.

Kahlil Gibran

"How are you holding up?" Cassie asks me.

"I'm okay, just trying to stay upbeat and think positive."

"Have either of the prescriptions helped any?"

"Well, I'm still losing hair, but there haven't been any large amounts lost during the past week. I don't know if it's because of the creams or if my follicles are just taking a brief pause."

"Well, hang in there. Giselle, the reason I'm calling is to ask if you would be my maid of honor."

"Really? I would love to," I answer, touched and honored that my future stepmother is asking me to stand with her.

"Thank you. Having you beside me when I marry your father means a lot."

"It means a lot to me, too," I say, wiping a tear away.

"And since Julian will be Jack's best man, everything will be perfect."

"It will, and he is honored as well. We're so happy for you guys," I say, grateful to have her in my life, and for the happiness she has brought to Dad.

We talk for a few minutes more and say goodbye.

I hang up the phone and stare out at the full moon through the kitchen window, allowing my thoughts to drift to and fro. I know it is only a matter of time before I lose the rest of my hair. I have accepted this fact, but a small hope is always there. I keep thinking I should go ahead and buy a couple of wigs, but it seems like there is always a reason to put it off. And I will definitely need one now that I am to be Cassie's maid of honor. Wearing a hat or scarf is completely out of the question.

Maybe tomorrow I will go and browse.

As soon as I awaken I can feel that something is different. Not wanting to wake Julian, I sit up, my hands immediately going to my head, and I am shocked to feel more bare sections on my scalp. Hesitantly, I go into the bathroom and close the door, locking it before turning on the light. I don't want to move to the mirror, afraid of what I will see, but I know I must, so I slowly approach the vanity with my eyes closed. Then I look at my reflection and a river of tears splash down my face. My scalp looks like patchwork. I have lost so much hair during the night no amount of camouflage will help.

Covering my mouth, I drop to the bench and cry.

"Giselle," Julian calls softly, "Swee'heart, would ye open the door?"

"I can't," I answer with a muffled cry.

"Please, darlin', tis' okay. I ken ye lost more, but it doesnae matter ta me. Ye are still the most bonnie lass I hav' ever seen. An' ye will alwa's be beautiful ta me no matter wha'. I know I keep repeatin' masel', but ye hav' ta believe me."

Hearing the emotion in his voice, I take another look at my reflection. There are small patches of dark hair left here and there. Heaving a resigned sigh, I wipe my face.

You will get through this. And this too shall pass. I get up and walk to the door.

"Julian?"

"Aye, honey.

"Would you do something for me?"

"Anythin', darlin'."

Taking a deep breath, I slowly open the door, a few more tears trailing down my cheeks. "Would you give me a haircut?" I slowly smile.

Julian pulls me into his arms, laughing and crying, raining kisses all over my face. "Aye. I would be glad ta giv' ye a haircut."

Five minutes later, he stands behind me with his hands on my shoulders as I examine my reflection. "So wha' do ye thin'?"

I hesitate, turning my head from left to right, and then smile. "I thin' ye took a bit too much o the top."

Laughing, he kneels beside me and holds me close. "Och, how I love ye, *mo nighean donn*."

"And I love you. Thank you, Julian."

"For wha'?"

"For being so good to me."

"Tis a privilege ta be able ta love ye, angel." He stands, his eyes meeting mine in the mirror, the burning passion in his gaze heating me to the core. "Now, forgiv' me, darlin', but I'm aboot ta take ye back ta bed for a wee bit an' hav' ma way with ye. All right?"

I stand and turn to him, wrapping my arms around his neck, and bury my fingers in his hair. "Aye. And you are definitely forgiven."

J. Adams

Chapter 14

A thing of beauty is a joy forever.

John Keats

I am beautiful. My hair does not make me. I am an amazing person with so much going for me. My husband loves and adores me and thinks I'm bonnie. That is all that matters.

Sitting at a vanity in the wig shop, I mentally repeat these affirmations and try on several wigs in various styles, but I am not happy with any of them. Of course, Julian tells me I look beautiful in each one and I tell him he's no help. He agrees and kisses my cheek. The sales woman brings in a few more styles for me to try. One of the wigs is very similar to my natural hair style. The silky black ringlets fall just past my shoulders and feel soft and luxurious. Julian whistles and my decision is made. I buy three of the style–two black and one, auburn. And as we leave the shop, I feel more beautiful than I have in a long time.

Julian decides to take me shopping so we head to the mall. Opening my car door, he takes my hand as I get out, keeping it in his as we move from store to store. We pick out a wedding gift for Dad and Cassie. Then I peruse the lingerie section in a department store and pick out Cassie's shower gift.

"I cannae wait ta see ye in tha'," Julian says, growling in my ear.

"Oh, I'll bet, but it's not for me," I say, blushing. "It's for Cassie."

He heaves a disappointed sigh. "If ye wan', I can hold yer place in line while ye go an' get another one for yersel'." He flashes a sexy mischievous grin.

"You mean for *you*," I tease and he nods.

"Oh, aye." He marches over and picks out one for me, placing it on the counter with the other. I just shake my head and smile. The cashier smiles as well and rings up our purchases. It isn't hard to guess what she's thinking.

"I need to stop in one more place," I say as we exit the store.

"Now, let me guess where yer goin' next." Julian rubs his chin like he is deep in thought. "Ah! The bookstore."

"How did you know?" I tease.

"Just luck."

"Makes me wonder if you have that leprechaun stowed away somewhere."

"Och, he's long gon' now. I gav' him a couple o bottles of whiskey from the pub an' I havnae seen him since."

Tsk, tsk, tsk. Nothing worse than a drunken leprechaun."

He grins. "Tell me aboot it."

Our bookstore is at the opposite end of the mall. The outside entrance is convenient, especially for parents bringing their children in for story time.

"Weel, why don' ye let me take the bags oot ta the car, an' while yer browsin' the books, I'll check oot another store for a bit."

"Sounds good. Give me about half an hour?"

"Sure. I'll plant masel' on the bench oot here by the kiosk." He kisses me and we hurry our separate ways.

"Good to see you, Giselle," Shawn, our young employee says as he finishes ringing up my books and puts them in a bag.

"It's good to see you, too. And thanks."

"You're welcome. And tell Julian to be prepared for the rush of mothers coming in tomorrow for his repeat performance at story time. They've all been going on about the gorgeous kilt-wearing Scotsman."

I laugh. "I'll be sure to tell him."

When I finally exit the store and meet Julian, I gasp, covering my mouth.

"Julian! What did you do?"

"Do ye like ma haircut, darlin'?" He stands and runs his fingers through the short tousled waves.

"I can't believe . . . but why?"

He smiles and places the tied ponytail in my hand. My bag slips from my fingers unheeded, and tears quickly blur my vision as he takes me in his arms.

"I didnae mean ta make ye cry, *mon nighean donn*."

I say nothing, but simply bury my face in his chest. I know why he did it, and the gesture touches me more than anything he has ever done. How I love this man! And how blessed I am that he loves me so much!

"Thank you," I finally whisper.

Drawing back a little, he takes my face in his hands, whispering against my lips, "I love ye more than anythin', ma bonnie, bonnie lassie," before covering my mouth and drinking deeply. Clinging to one another, we are completely in a world of our own. A world where love, passion and complete adoration consumes our hearts and our souls. A world nothing can penetrate, and our devotion to one another is all that matters.

Dad whistles as we enter the house. "You're beautiful as usual."

"Tell me aboot it," Julian says, placing the bags on the sofa.

"And Julian, you look like a new man."

Julian smiles, lifting my hand to his lips. "No new, just different. I'm the same man, the one who desperately loves yer daughter."

J. Adams

I wrap my arms around his waist, gazing up at him with eyes full of love and adoration, secure in the knowledge that no matter what trials may come, no matter how hard emotional storms may rage, I will be able to face them all and overcome, with Julian, my husband and Scottish knight, at my side.

Epilogue

Beauty is how you feel inside, and it reflects in your eyes. It is not something physical.

Sophia Loren

The wedding is held in the back yard of our home. I wipe a tear away as Dad and Cassie stand before the reverend and repeat their vows, pledging to love and honor one another. Cassie is a beautiful bride in her silky white princess gown. And Dad's black tux looks like it was made just for him. He is indeed a handsome groom. In attendance are my grandparents and some of Dad's friends and employees.

Julian and I share meaningful glances throughout the ceremony, remembering our wedding ceremonies, both in the states and in Scotland. No words are needed as our eyes clearly speak our love to one another.

Two hours later, after hugs, kisses, and more tears are shed, Julian and I stand at the curb and wave as we watch Dad and Cassie drive away, heading toward their new life.

Six weeks later

Castle Urquhart

Loch Ness, Scotland

Standing in the tower of the castle ruins, with Julian's arms around my waist, we gaze through the window at Loch Ness. Even shrouded in the thick fog, this place feels magical. Battles were fought over Castle Urquhart, but in the end, Scotland regained her treasure, and I am awed to again be standing amidst such history.

"The first time I brought ye here, I thought ta masel', 'I wan' ta marry this woman right here, right now.' But I couldnae deprive ye o a weddin'."

I smile, turning in his arms. "And I appreciate your thoughtfulness. Though, if truth be told, I would have married you with only the reverend and nature as witnesses. I wanted you as desperately as you wanted me." I softly touch my lips to his. "I still do."

"Aye." His voice is husky. "My wan' for ye willnae ever stop. When I am in ma grave, I will still burn for ye." He kisses me, whispering against my lips. "Ye hav' no idea o the power ye hav' over me."

A delightful shiver causes goose bumps to cover my arms as his hands caress my waist and back. "I have some idea, because I feel the same. From the moment you first looked into my eyes when you sang, I have felt a connection to you that only grows stronger and deeper with each day that passes. There are times that I still wonder how you can be mine, and what I did to deserve you."

"Ah, darlin', ye take ma own thoughts an' give voice ta them." He holds me close, caressing my brow with his lips. "Ye donnae ken, an' I've never said, but almost every night since we married, I awaken for a wee moment an' just look at ye. I look at yer beloved body an' marvel tha' ye belong ta me, tha' we are one flesh. I gaze at yer face, committin' ta memory every plane, every contour, thankin' God for the marvels o the human senses. An' then I touch ye, an' I am infused with renewed joy."

Julian has always been a romantic, but his words take me by complete surprise. His devotion is so beautiful I can't come up with anything original that would be worthy of him. I turn back around and face the sea, my arms wrapped over his. One of my favorite poetic pieces by Pierre Choderlos De Laclos comes to mind.

"*Loved and respected by a husband I love and respect, my duties and my pleasures are combined. I am happy and I ought to be. If there exist more acute pleasures I do not want to know them. Is there a sweeter pleasure than to be at peace with oneself? . . . What you call happiness is but a turmoil of the senses, a tempest of passions which it is frightening to witness even from the safety of the shore . . .*"

"Amen, love."

We say nothing more for a long while, we simply soak in the view. Soon the mist over Loch Ness slowly lifts, and for a moment I think I see . . .

No, it couldn't be . . . "Julian!" I say, never taking my eyes away from the area of water I've been staring at. "Was that . . . do you think . . . ?"

"In these enchantin' waters, anythin's possible." He takes my hand. "Let's go an' hav' a closer look."

Hand in hand, we leave the castle, me and my knight—the owner and protector of my heart—wielding a warrior's unconditional love as his sword, and unending devotion as his shield.

William Wallace would indeed be proud.

Afterword

Though this story is fiction, Alopecia is very real and emotionally painful. I have been dealing with this dreaded condition for years and getting progressively worse.

But you know what? It is okay. I am in a good place with the reality of it. Of course, I still have days every now and then when I feel less attractive, but I quickly pull myself out of the mire, less it swallows me completely.

I am fortunate enough to have a husband who tells me I am beautiful every day, and I am grateful to him for loving me unconditionally. I know when the day finally comes that my hair is completely gone and I have to wear wigs full time, his love for me won't change, ansd because of that, I will continue to be okay. My wig collection will just expand and I will be one of the most stylish women around.

That thought makes me smile.

About Alopecia

Alopecia areata is a common autoimmune skin disease resulting in the loss of hair on the scalp and elsewhere on the body. It usually starts with one or more small, round, smooth patches on the scalp and can progress to total scalp hair loss (alopecia totalis) or complete body hair loss (alopecia universalis). Alopecia areata affects approximately two percent of the population overall, including more than 5 million people in the United States alone. This common skin disease is highly unpredictable and cyclical. Hair can grow back in or fall out again at any time, and the disease course is different for each person.

National Alopecia Areata Foundation

NAAF was established in 1981 with one clear goal; to offer support to individuals affected by alopecia areata. Though the mission has expanded over the past two decades, the importance of providing a substantial support program to people of all ages and interests has not diminished.

To learn more about Alopecia and find a support group, visit the NAAF website at www.naaf.org.

About the Author

J. (Jewel) Adams stays crazy busy with her family and writing. She has written several books in different genres, mainly romance, and is also a motivational speaker to both youth and adult audiences.

She is on the last leg of home schooling her two youngest, and between that and conjuring up new ideas for her books, her brain cells are on overload most of the time. She and her husband Sean are the parents of eight children and grandparents to five and counting.

In her spare time (when she has any) she likes to curl up with a good book and a healthy stash of orange Tic Tacs. She and her family reside in Utah.

Jewel loves hearing from her fans, so if you would like to contact her to tell her how much you love her books or give her sympathy for the fried brain cells, contact her at jewela40@gmail.com

To check out Jewel's other books, visit her website at **JewelAdams.com**

And stop by her blog: **jewelsbestgems.blogspot.com**

Other books by J. Adams/Jewel Adams
Still His Woman
The Legacy
The Wishing Hour
Tears of Heaven
Place In This World
The Journey
Against the Odds
Mercedes' Mountain
Guardian of My Heart
Sweet 21 Birthday Ball

Ebooks
The Wishing Hour
The Legacy
Tears of Heaven
Place In This World: The Sequel to The Journey
The Journey
Mercedes' Mountain
That Kind of Love
The Shelter of His Arms
What the Heart Sees
The Sound of Love
Stories of the Heart
Against the Odds
Guardian of My Heart
Elise's Heart
For Love of Angel
Sweet 21 Birthday Ball
Say What You Need to Say

Children's Book
Forbidden Portals: The Quicksilver Project